D06617459

For Isabelle Hudson,
with lots of love and
fairy sparkles

Special thanks to
Sue Mongredien

ORCHARD BOOKS
338 Euston Road, London NW1 3BH
Orchard Books Australia
Level 17/207 Kent Street, Sydney, NSW 2000
A Paperback Original

First published in 2009 by Orchard Books.

© 2009 Rainbow Magic Limited.
A HIT Entertainment company. Rainbow Magic
is a trademark of Rainbow Magic Limited.
Reg. U.S. Pat. & Tm. Off. And other countries.

Illustrations © Orchard Books 2009

A CIP catalogue record for this book is available
from the British Library.

ISBN 978 1 40830 349 8
1 3 5 7 9 10 8 6 4 2

Printed in China by Imago

Orchard Books is a division of Hachette Children's Books,
an Hachette UK company

www.hachette.co.uk

Ashley the Dragon Fairy

by Daisy Meadows

ORCHARD BOOKS

www.rainbowmagic.co.uk

The Fairyland Palace
Barn
Farmhouse
Stables
Clubhouse
CAMP
Adventure Lake
Birdwatching Tower

Jack Frost's
Ice Castle
Meadows
Amphitheatre
The Labyrinth
Maze of tunnels
Cabins
Waterfall
Hills

There are seven special animals,
Who live in Fairyland.
They use their magic powers
To help others where they can.

A dragon, black cat, firebird,
A seahorse and snow swan too,
A unicorn and ice bear -
I know just what to do.

I'll lock them in my castle
And never let them out.
The world will turn more miserable,
Of that, I have no doubt...

Contents

The Adventure Begins!	9
Off to Fairyland!	21
Into the Labyrinth	37
Searching for Sizzle	49
The Pogwurzel Plan	55
Fairy Flying	63

The Adventure Begins!

"Bye, Mum, bye, Dad!" Kirsty Tate yelled, waving as her parents' car pulled away.

Her mum, who was in the passenger seat, rolled down the window. "See you next week," she called. "And have a wonderful time, both of you!"

Kirsty grinned at her best friend, Rachel Walker. "We will!" both girls chorused.

A whole week away at an outdoor adventure camp – it was going to be just perfect!

"Hi guys," came a voice from behind them. They turned to see a tall, smiling girl with long brown hair, whose red T-shirt had "Adventure Camp Counsellor" printed on in yellow letters. "You must be Kirsty and Rachel," she said. "I'm Lucy, one of the counsellors here. I'll take you to your cabin, OK?"

Kirsty and Rachel followed Lucy along a path, feeling very excited. They passed through a small wooded area where Rachel spotted a squirrel bounding up one of the pine trees, and then out to a sunny meadow with rolling hills beyond it. There were wooden cabins dotted here and there, each with colourful curtains at the window, and brightly painted front doors. Music floated from some of the cabins, and Kirsty and Rachel could see clusters of other campers having fun. There was a basketball ring attached to one of the trees and a group of boys were shooting hoops. A couple of girls were messing about on skateboards outside another cabin, laughing and chatting.

"Here we are," Lucy said just then, veering away to a cabin on the right. It had a light blue door and blue gingham curtains at the windows. "I'll let you unpack, then I suggest you explore the camp to get your bearings. There are maps everywhere, so you won't get lost. We'll all be going on a caving trip in about an hour, OK?"

Kirsty and Rachel thanked Lucy, then entered the cabin feeling curious and excited about their home for the next week.

There was a bunk bed and four single beds, a separate bathroom and a couple of posters on the walls. Rachel hurled herself onto the lower bunk and Kirsty dumped her cardigan on the top bunk to bag it.

"Wow, look at this," Kirsty said, spotting a timetable. "Canoeing, horse-riding, swimming… There's so much to do here!"

"I can't wait to meet the other girls in our cabin," Rachel said, smiling.

"And you never know… We might even make some new fairy friends while we're here, too!"

Kirsty beamed at the thought. She and Rachel were good friends with the fairies, and they'd had lots of adventures with them. Magical things just seemed to happen whenever the two of them got together! "Come on, let's explore," she suggested. "We can unpack later. I'm dying to look around!"

Rachel agreed, and the girls left their bags and headed out into the sunshine again.

There was a large building in the centre of the campsite with a sign above the double doors that read "Clubhouse". Near to it was a wooden signpost with arrows pointing in different directions – one said "Canteen", another read "Sports Pitches" and a third said "Outdoor Amphitheatre".

"Look, there's a map here," Rachel said, pointing to a colourful sign in a glass case, just outside the clubhouse. She and Kirsty strolled over to it.

"Ooh, a waterfall," Kirsty said, showing Rachel on the map.

"And there are the stables," Rachel noticed. She blinked. The sun was shining very brightly onto the glass case, making it sparkle. She shielded her eyes. Suddenly the light seemed dazzling!

Kirsty was blinking and looking away too. "The sun is so strong," she commented. "I wish I had my sunglasses!"

Rachel was about to reply when another voice was heard. "Kirsty! Rachel! This is King Oberon. The fairies need your help. Please use your magic lockets to come to Fairyland as soon as you can!"

Rachel gasped. So the sparkling light from the glass case was fairy magic! She grabbed Kirsty's hand and pulled her around the side of the clubhouse, where nobody could see them.

"Come on," she said, fiddling with the catch of the special locket she always wore around her neck. "Oh, I hope the fairies are all right!"

Kirsty was busy with her own locket. Inside there was some magical fairy dust, given to them by the fairy queen herself. They each took a pinch and sprinkled it over themselves, then held hands as a magical sparkly whirlwind began spinning around them. Another fairy adventure was beginning!

Moments later, the girls felt themselves being gently set down, and the whirlwind spun away. They blinked and looked around. "The Fairyland Palace!" Kirsty cried in delight, seeing it in front of them.

"And there are Queen Titania and King Oberon," Rachel realised. "Come on!"

The two friends ran over to the fairy king and queen, who were standing with a group of other fairies that the girls didn't recognise. As usual, Rachel and Kirsty had shrunk down to fairy-size now that they were in Fairyland.

"Hello again, Kirsty and Rachel," King Oberon said. He didn't seem his usual cheerful self, Kirsty noticed, and she wondered why.

"We've called you here because unfortunately Jack Frost is up to his tricks again. This time he's really gone too far! He's stolen seven Magical Animals from our fairies –

a dragon, a black cat, a firebird, a seahorse, a snow swan, a unicorn and an ice bear."

"Why?" Rachel asked. "What does he want with them?"

Queen Titania joined in the conversation. "These are our Magical Animal Fairies," she said, pointing to the group of seven fairies who stood with her. "And every Spring, they get seven new young Magical Animals to look

after and train for one year. Each Magical Animal has special qualities and helps spread the kind of magic that every human and fairy can possess – the magic of imagination, luck, humour, friendship, compassion, healing and courage. The fairies spend a whole year teaching the baby animals how to use and control their powers."

Kirsty felt she still didn't quite understand and was about to ask a question when one of the Magical Animal Fairies stepped forwards. Her hair was in an afro style and she wore combat trousers, embroidered with a dragon on one leg, and a stripy vest top. "Hi there," she said. "I'm Ashley the Dragon Fairy, and this is Lara the Black Cat Fairy, Erin the Firebird Fairy,

Rihanna the Seahorse Fairy, Sophia the Snow Swan Fairy, Leona the Unicorn Fairy and Caitlin the Ice Bear Fairy."

Rachel and Kirsty smiled at the seven friendly faces before them. "Hi," Rachel said, curious to know more about these fairies and their animals.

"Each of the Magical Animals looks after a different magical power," Ashley went on. "The baby dragon is responsible for imagination. The black cat looks after luck, the firebird's magical quality is humour and the seahorse is responsible for friendship. The snow swan inspires compassion, the baby unicorn has the power of healing, and the ice bear looks after the power of courage."

"We spend a whole year teaching the baby animals how to use and control their magical powers," Lara added. "Once the Magical Animals are all trained, they go back to their families in Fairyland, where they will help spread their magical gifts throughout the fairy world and the human world."

"But Jack Frost kidnapped the

Magical Animals because he didn't want them to be fully trained," the queen explained. "And if the animals aren't trained, they can't help spread their lovely magical qualities, like imagination and humour – qualities that everyone needs!"

"Jack Frost would like the world to be as miserable as he is," the King added. "He doesn't want people or fairies to have friendship and luck."

Kirsty and Rachel exchanged horrified glances. They couldn't imagine how awful life would be without friendship! And the idea of a world without any humour or courage was too sad for words.

"We'll help," Kirsty said at once. "We'll go to Jack Frost's castle right away and get the young animals back for you!"

The King smiled. "Thank you, Kirsty," he said. "We knew we could count on you and Rachel. However, something remarkable has happened. Come to the Seeing Pool and we can show you."

The King and Queen led the girls and the Magical Animal Fairies to a large blue pool in the palace gardens.

The Queen touched the surface of the water with her wand and it shimmered with all the colours of the rainbow.

A picture started to form on the water – a picture of Jack Frost surrounded by all of the Magical Animals outside his Ice Castle. Rachel giggled as she saw the little dragon sneeze and blast out some flames, melting a part of the icy wall!

"Oh dear," she said. "I don't think Jack Frost will be pleased about that."

"Look at the ice bear!" Kirsty said, pointing to a different area of the picture. A cute white bear was chasing Jack Frost's goblin servants and making them freeze into icy statues by tapping them with its paws.

The girls watched the scene develop into chaos. The Magical Animals were now happily chasing each other around the castle, completely ignoring Jack Frost's orders. And then, suddenly, a sparkling window opened up in one of the castle walls and the seven young animals slipped through it, one after another.

"Where have they gone?" Rachel asked, puzzled.

"Into the human world, it seems," the Queen told her. "And there's Jack Frost sending his goblins through the same window, to track them down!"

The girls watched the picture as a group of the goblin servants scrambled through the magical window and vanished from sight. The window gradually faded away.

"What happened next?" Kirsty asked.

Ashley shrugged unhappily. "We don't know," she said. "The animals must be hiding somewhere in the human world."

"We've got to find them, before anyone else does," Erin added. "They're so young, they can't control their magical abilities – and they may be causing strange things to happen in the human world!"

"We'll help you find them," Rachel said at once.

"Thank you," said King Oberon. "But you must be careful. As Erin said, the animals aren't able to work their magic very well yet. This might mean that their magical qualities of imagination, luck, humour, friendship, compassion, healing and courage are more powerful than usual. It might even mean that the qualities work in reverse if the animals are nervous."

"The magical qualities will affect anyone who comes near the animals," the Queen said. "So watch out for anybody acting strangely – it may lead you to one of them."

"I'll come to the human world with you to search for Sizzle, the baby dragon," Ashley said. "He's got a cold at the moment – he must have caught it while he was at Jack Frost's Ice Castle. I'm a bit worried about him."

"You must be careful, and stay out of sight," the Queen reminded her. "No one in the human world can know about Fairyland or anyone who lives here. Good luck!"

With those words, she pointed her wand at Ashley, Kirsty and Rachel.

The three of them just had time to call goodbye before another glittery whirlwind whisked them up and took them spinning through the air…

Into the Labyrinth

With a last flurry of sparkles, the girls found themselves back to their usual size, and in the Adventure Camp once again. Ashley looked about eagerly, her gauzy wings shimmering in the sunshine – but then a look of disappointment crossed her face. "We Magical Animal Fairies can always sense when our creatures are nearby," she said, "but I'm not picking up anything here."

She was about to say something else when they heard voices. Ashley darted onto Kirsty's shoulder and hid behind her hair, not wanting to be seen.

"I guess we'd better go back to our cabin," Rachel said. "It must be time to go on the caving trip."

"Keep a look out for dragons," Kirsty whispered excitedly, as they headed off. Oh, it was so wonderful to be starting a new fairy adventure!

Back at their cabin, they saw that their room-mates had now arrived and were all unpacking. "Hi," said a blonde girl wearing a pink baseball cap. "I'm Emma, and this is Katie, Natasha and Catherine."

"I'm Rachel and this is Kirsty," Rachel replied.

"Hi," Kirsty said to them all. She could feel Ashley still tucked under her hair and hoped that none of the other girls would spot the little fairy!

Just then, Lucy popped her head around the door. "Hi everyone, it's time to set off on our trip," she said.

"We're going to the Labyrinth – some hidden caves deep in the mountain. It'll be cold in there so make sure you wear warm clothes under your waterproofs and thick socks with your walking boots. Oh, and bring some gloves, too!"

The six girls quickly got ready. While everyone was busy, Ashley nipped out from her hiding place and tucked herself into the front pocket of Rachel's coat.

"Hey, what's that?" Natasha asked just then, and Rachel's heart almost stopped, thinking she must have spotted Ashley.

But Natasha was pointing to Rachel's bed, and she saw with a huge rush of relief that Natasha meant a magazine which had fallen out of her bag.

"Oh…it's a new magazine," Rachel replied thankfully. "You can borrow it later if you like."

"Thanks," Natasha said, looking pleased. "Are we all ready, then? Let's go to the Labyrinth!"

The six girls went out to meet the rest of the campers.

Lucy and some of the other camp counsellors handed out helmets with lights fixed to the front and they all set off together through the campsite.

After a short walk, they arrived at the caves. "I'll just do a quick head count to make sure we've got everyone," Lucy said as they gathered at the entrance. She walked around, counting under her breath. "Nineteen, twenty, twenty-one..."

She frowned. "That's weird. I thought we'd only have eighteen people here. Have I counted wrong?"

She took a large red rucksack off her back and rummaged through it, pulling out a register. "I'll call out the names, then we can see who we've got," she decided. "Emily Adams?"

As Lucy went through the register, Kirsty noticed a group of campers sneaking off into the cave! "Rachel," she hissed. "Look!"

Rachel's eyes widened. "I'm sure I saw a flash of green," she whispered. "They must be goblins!"

Ashley peered over the top of Rachel's pocket to see. "Why are they going into the cave?" she wondered in her tiny silvery voice.

"Kirsty Tate?" called Lucy just then.

"Here!" Kirsty replied.

"And Rachel Walker," Lucy said.

"Here," Rachel said.

Lucy looked relieved. "OK – that's everyone," she said. "I must have been having a dippy moment when I was counting. Let's go into the Labyrinth!"

The group went into the mountainside, along a rocky tunnelled path that led out into a huge, high cavern. It was very eerie. Their voices echoed against the cave walls and they could hear water dripping in the distance. "These are limestone caves," one of the counsellors told the group, shining her torch up to the roof of the cavern. "Up there are what's called stalactites – do you see? They look rather like rock icicles."

"And if you think they're impressive, wait until we get to the maze," another counsellor added. "There are tunnels after tunnels after tunnels – and just as you're starting to feel really lost, you come out into this magnificent cave full of the most enormous stalactites you've ever seen."

Lucy, meanwhile, was unzipping her jacket. "It's warm in here," she said in surprise. "Usually it's much cooler than this. And wetter too – but the

path isn't slippery at all today, is it? I'm even going to take my gloves off!"

Rachel looked down and saw that Lucy was right. The rocky ground beneath their feet looked bone dry except for... She frowned and bent lower to take a closer look. There on the ground was a set of tiny, clawed footprints – and they were shimmering with magic!

"Kirsty, Ashley," she hissed, her voice trembling with excitement. "Look – I think the baby dragon may have come this way!"

Ashley's face lit up with a grin. "That is definitely a dragon's trail. Sizzle must have been here!" she whispered. "And that explains why the cave is so warm: dragons give off lots of heat, especially if they have a cold and keep sneezing out flames!"

"So that's why the goblins are here, too," Kirsty worked out. "They must be looking for Sizzle. I hope they haven't found him yet."

"Can you all get into small groups, please?" Lucy called at that moment. "We're going to have a race now, and the first team to reach the centre of the Labyrinth wins. Watch out for the uneven floors, and no running! Ready, steady...go!"

The campers all headed off into the maze of tunnels. Rachel and Kirsty struck out alone with Ashley, who flew out of her hiding place to flutter alongside them. If Sizzle was somewhere in the caves, they had to find the dragon before the goblins or any of the campers got to him!

"Oh!" Rachel gasped suddenly. She stopped and pointed at the wall ahead. There they could see the shadow of a goblin's big nose and the safety helmet he wore on his head. "He must be just around the corner," she whispered, feeling her heart thud a little faster.

She, Kirsty and Ashley moved towards the shadow. But the goblin must have heard the girls' footsteps because he began running, just managing to stay out of their reach as he pelted through the tunnels.

Kirsty noticed a series of black marks along the walls as they went by. "These are strange," she said, and ran a finger along one of them. It came away black with soot.

"They must be scorch marks from Sizzle's sneezes," Ashley guessed. "We're getting closer to him!"

The girls could hear the voices of the other campers coming from the nearby tunnels. Then, as they turned around a corner, they bumped straight into a group of three goblins – and they all fell over at once.

Kirsty and Rachel scrambled to their feet, as did the goblins. Ashley perched on Kirsty's shoulder, looking wary.

The goblins seemed a bit jumpy about something. "It's only silly girls," one of them muttered, his face a paler shade of green than normal. "Nothing scary."

Another goblin scowled. "I wasn't scared," he blustered. "Anyway, come on, we've got work to do. We're on a dragon hunt! And we're going to catch it before any of those interfering fairies!"

Rachel and Kirsty exchanged anxious glances, both thinking frantically. They had to think of a way to stop the goblins getting to Sizzle!

Luckily, a brilliant idea popped into Rachel's head and she winked at Kirsty, hoping her friend would play along with her. "Be careful, then," she said meaningfully, speaking directly to the goblin who looked particularly pale and nervous. "Because you get lots of Pogwurzels in these caves, you know."

The goblins stared. "Pogwurzels?" they echoed, their eyes dark with fear.

Rachel and Kirsty both knew that there were no such creatures as Pogwurzels – but goblin mothers often told naughty goblin children that if they didn't behave, a Pogwurzel would come and get them.

Lots of younger goblins still believed in Pogwurzels – and were very scared of them!

Kirsty hid a smile as she joined the conversation. "Didn't you know?" she asked the goblins. "Pogwurzels love caves. They like being in dark, scary places – especially if there are goblins to chase."

While Kirsty was talking, Rachel asked Ashley in a whisper if she would fly around the corner. "And when you hear me shout the word 'Pogwurzel', make a really scary sound!" she added.

Ashley grinned. "Leave it to me," she whispered back, and slipped away unnoticed.

Then Rachel pretended to gasp in surprise. "Look – what's that?" she cried in a frightened voice, pointing behind the goblins. "I think I just saw one!"

The goblins turned in fright, clutching at each other and looking very scared.

"And there's another!" Kirsty cried, pointing into a shadowy corner.

"I want my mummy," whimpered one of the goblins, staring around nervously.

"I want to go home!" cried another, his lower lip wobbling.

"There's a Pogwurzel!" Rachel yelled in a loud voice – and right on cue, Ashley used her magic to create a ferocious-sounding roar!

"Help!" shrieked the goblins, scattering from the cave. "Let's get out of here!"

Ashley fluttered back to the girls, grinning in delight.

"That worked brilliantly," she said. "Well done – what an imaginative idea! Now let's keep searching. I can sense Sizzle is close by, in the centre of the maze."

"Great – what are we waiting for?" Kirsty said eagerly. "Let's get through this maze as soon as we can!"

Unfortunately, it wasn't quite as easy as that. The girls kept jogging through the tunnels but found dead end after dead end. The rocky walls looked so similar, it was difficult to get their bearings, and after a few minutes they felt completely lost.

Just as Kirsty was starting to despair, they heard a loud sneeze. "Bless you!" she said automatically and then smiled. "Hey – might that be Sizzle?" But then she frowned. Something strange seemed to be happening to her. It felt as if all her ideas and imagination were draining away. Everything seemed grey in her mind.

Rachel was also feeling peculiar. She shook her head. "Something's wrong," she said anxiously. "It's as if a light bulb has been switched off in my mind. I know we should be thinking about what to do next…but nothing's happening in my brain."

"Me too," Kirsty said, clutching the sides of her head. "Why can't we think properly? This is horrible!"

"I think I know what's happening," Ashley said. "Don't worry – it's Sizzle who's causing this. Because he's nervous, his powers are working in reverse and so your imagination is disappearing temporarily."

Almost as soon as she'd finished speaking, that all changed. Suddenly, ideas were pouring into the girls' heads, almost faster than they could think.

"Hey – I know what we could do!" Kirsty said, beaming.

"Oh yes – I've just had a great idea how we can help Sizzle, too," Rachel said excitedly.

Ashley chuckled. "It looks as though Sizzle's magical powers are working properly again, and boosting your imagination!" she said.

It wasn't just Kirsty and Rachel who were full of ideas. In the tunnels all around them they could hear other campers talking excitedly. "I've thought of a brilliant story about being here in the cave," a girl in the next tunnel said.

"A song about a funny cave-monster has just popped into my head," laughed a boy in delight nearby.

"You could make up a cool ghost story set in these caves," a third person said.

"Everyone's getting closer to Sizzle and the centre of the maze," Kirsty realised. "We've got to find him quickly, before anyone else does!"

Ashley nodded. "I'll turn you into fairies," she said, waving her wand over them. "That way we can all fly together and go much quicker!"

Green fairy dust swirled around Kirsty and Rachel and they found themselves shrinking smaller and smaller, until they were the same size as Ashley. They were fairies again! Kirsty fluttered her wings and zoomed into the air. "What are we waiting for?" she cried. "Let's go!"

The three fairy friends flew at top speed through the maze. All around, they could hear pounding footsteps and excited laughter as the other campers tried to find the middle.

Luckily, the fairies could go much faster than anyone else! Within a few moments they'd reached the maze's centre – and there was a small green scaly dragon hovering in mid-air, with black puffs of smoke coming from his nostrils.

"Sizzle!" cried Ashley happily.

At the sound of her voice, his ears pricked up – and a big smile spread across his face as he saw his fairy mistress.

Sizzle raced through the air towards her, growing smaller and smaller as he did so. By the time he reached Ashley, he was tiny and able to leap into her arms for a cuddle.

"Oh, he's so cute!" cried Rachel in delight, flying over to pet him. Kirsty couldn't resist either, and Sizzle made the funniest little roaring purrs they had ever heard.

"We must be nearly there now," a voice rang out just then. "Hurry – I think it's this way!"

The fairies exchanged anxious glances. The campers were approaching. Ashley quickly waved her wand over Kirsty and Rachel, and with a flood of glittery sparkles, they were turned back into girls.

"Thank you so much," Ashley said hastily. "Now I can take Sizzle back to Fairyland and finish his training. I'd better fly!"

In a last shower of fairy dust, she was gone – just as Lucy emerged from one of the tunnels. "Kirsty, Rachel, well done!" she cried, smiling. "You're the first ones here. No one's ever made it to the centre so fast before! How did you manage to find your way so quickly?"

Other boys and girls were now pouring into the central area from the different tunnels around the cave – all chatting and laughing happily.

Kirsty and Rachel shared a knowing look. "I guess we just used our imagination," Kirsty replied.

"It was really good fun," Rachel added truthfully. She gave Kirsty a secret smile as Lucy went off to talk to some of the other campers. The holiday was already shaping up to be very exciting … and with six of the young Magical Animals left to find, the girls were sure there were plenty more adventures to come!

Ashley the Dragon Fairy has got her Magical Animal back! Now Rachel and Kirsty must help...

Lara the Black Cat Fairy

"Come on, Kirsty." Rachel Walker picked up her rucksack and smiled at her best friend, Kirsty Tate. "It's time for our next activity – we're going on an orienteering expedition."

"Oh, great!" Kirsty exclaimed happily, lacing up her walking boots. "I'm really looking forward to it." Then she grinned. "To be honest, I'm not exactly sure what an orienteering expedition is, though!"

Rachel and the other girls in the cabin, Emma, Natasha, Katie and Catherine, smiled warmly at Kirsty.

"Orienteering is using a compass and a map to find your way to a meeting-place," Emma explained. "All the different teams try to get there first. It's great fun."

"It sounds fantastic," Kirsty agreed.

"I've enjoyed every activity here at camp so far," Rachel remarked to Kirsty, as their room-mates went outside.

Kirsty nodded. "And it's been even *more* exciting since our fairy friends asked for our help!" she whispered.

On the day the girls arrived at the camp, they discovered that Jack Frost had been up to his old tricks in Fairyland again. This time, he and his naughty goblin servants had kidnapped seven Magical Animals from the Magical Animal Fairies.

The Magical Animals were very rare

and precious because they helped to spread the kind of magic that every human and fairy could possess – the magic of imagination, luck, humour, friendship, compassion, healing and courage. The fairies trained the Magical Animals for a whole year to make sure they knew how to use their powers to spread their wonderful gifts throughout the human and the fairy worlds.

But Jack Frost was determined to make sure that the animals never got the chance to use their magical gifts. He wanted everyone to be as grumpy and miserable as him! So he and his goblins had stolen the young Magical Animals and taken them to his Ice Castle. But the animals had managed to escape into the human world, where they had hidden themselves away. Jack Frost had sent his goblins after them, but Rachel and Kirsty, with the help of the Magical Animal Fairies, were determined to find the young animals first, and return them safely to Fairyland...

Read the rest of

Lara

the Black Cat Fairy

to find out what magic happens next...